Approved!

ISBN 978-1532860133
Pleasant Green Books

Approved!

A Story About
Quaker Meeting for Business

By
Nancy L. Haines
Illustrated by Anne E.G. Nydam

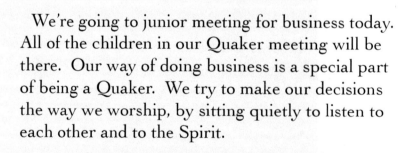

We're going to junior meeting for business today. All of the children in our Quaker meeting will be there. Our way of doing business is a special part of being a Quaker. We try to make our decisions the way we worship, by sitting quietly to listen to each other and to the Spirit.

We start our meeting with silence. This quiet time reminds us to settle down just like we do at meeting for worship. Sometimes the younger children get wiggly, so we have paper for them so they can color quietly and still be a part of our community.

Lilah is the clerk of junior meeting for business. We call her a clerk because she leads the meetings and helps us as we make decisions.

The clerk reads us the agenda. The agenda is a list of the work we have to do at the meeting. Today we are going to decide what to do with the money that we made selling hot dogs after meeting last Sunday. We had a lot of fun and everyone in the meeting said they liked our hot dogs.

Agen...
Hot dog
Other business

Liam is our treasurer. He keeps track of how much money we have. He stands and says that we have $97.60.

We want to use the money to help others. Lilah asks where we should give the money.

Sarah raises her hand. When Lilah calls on her, she stands and says that the money should go to take care of animals. We sit in silence to think about what she said. We try to listen to God within each other.

Emmett wants to speak next. He stands and says that we should give the money to an orphanage in Kenya. His older brother went to a work camp at the orphanage last summer and told us about the children who live there. We get quiet again to think about what Emmett says.

Other children tell about other ideas, and we think about each of them. Sometimes we have to listen to God and to each other for a long time until we know what is best for our community.

The littlest girl in our group has been very quiet. She raises her hand and says that she wants to help children who don't have families.

Lilah looks around and sees the smiles. She sees that everyone is excited about giving the money to the orphanage. Lilah has discerned or figured out the sense of the meeting.

She says, "I see that we are all happy about giving the money to help children who are orphans."

Sarah really wanted to give the money to help animals, but she knows that helping Kenyan children is right for our group. She is in unity with the discernment of the meeting.

Agenda
Hot dog money
Other business

Agenda
Hot dog money
Other business

Jared is our recording clerk. His job is to write down the decisions that we make. What he writes is called a minute. We sit quietly while Jared writes about giving money to the orphanage. He reads the minute to us, "Junior meeting for business will give the money from our hot dog sales to the orphanage in Kenya."

Liam wants to say something about this minute. He says, "Clerk, please," to get Lilah's attention. He stands and says that we should save some of the money to buy more hot dogs so we can have another sale. He suggests that we donate $50. We nod our heads.

Jared changes the minute to match our new understanding: "Junior meeting for business will give $50 from our hot dog sales to the orphanage in Kenya."

Lilah asks if this minute is the right way to say what we decided. We all shout, "Approved!" We're glad we took the time to listen carefully to each other and to the Spirit.

We end junior meeting for business with a moment of silence. Then we shake each other's hands to let us know that business meeting is over.

We race out to the playground. Children of all ages play together. We know each other better because we have learned to work together in meeting for business. We are a community!

Queries
Some Questions to Think About

Do you come to junior meeting for business as often as you can? Are you ready to participate in the meeting?

Are you willing to listen carefully when others speak?

Do you know that your ideas are important and that you should speak up when you have something helpful to say? Are you willing to accept that your idea may not be the best for your community?

When your clerk is trying to figure out the sense of the meeting, do you sit quietly and try to listen to God within each other?

Do you remain silent while the clerks are trying to write a minute? Do you accept the minute with joy when it says what the group has discerned?

Do you welcome all children in your meeting and work together to create a loving community?

Glossary
Useful Quaker Definitions

Quakers believe there is something of God in everyone.
The children in this story refer to God or the Spirit.   Other Quakers
call this the Inner Light, Inward Teacher, or Christ Within.

CENTERING – We start meetings by sitting quietly to let go of distractions so that we may better listen to the Spirit.

CLERK – The clerk is the person responsible for organizing the agenda and conducting the meeting. The clerk also helps the group figure out the sense of the meeting and helps us discover what God wants us to do.

CONSENSUS – Some people say that Quakers use consensus which means finding a decision that is acceptable to each person. In meeting for business, we try to find the sense of the meeting which is a decision that belongs to the whole group.

CONCERN – We sometimes have a special interest in a spiritual or social matter which might lead to action. In this story, Emmett brings a concern for the orphanage in Kenya.

DISCERNMENT – Discernment is a way of listening to God and one another in order to sense what is the best decision for the community.

QUERIES – Quakers often use questions to help us focus on the things that are spiritually important. This book has queries to help us prepare for meeting for business.

MEETING FOR BUSINESS – Quakers come together in worship to make decisions and to think about the issues that affect our community. Some Quakers call this a "meeting for worship with attention to business" to remind us that we listen to the Spirit as well as each other.

MINUTE – The clerk will say what he or she thinks is the sense of the meeting. The recording clerk will then write a statement of what has been decided. The minute can then be approved by the group. Sometimes, the minute will say that we are not ready to make a decision.

QUAKER PROCESS – Quakers make decisions in a worshipful manner by sitting quietly and listening to each other and to the Spirit.

RECORDING CLERK – The recording clerk writes down the minute and may change it until the group agrees that it is the right way to say what has been decided. The minute is saved so that we can read it in the future.

SEASONING – Quakers will take time to make sure that a decision is right for the group. Sometimes, everyone will agree that we need to wait until another meeting to make a good decision.

SENSE OF THE MEETING – The sense of the meeting is an agreement about what decision the group has reached in its discernment. Sometimes, the sense may be that the meeting is not ready to decide.

UNITY – Unity is reached when everyone agrees that a decision is best for the group after listening to each other and to the Spirit. If a person had hoped for a different idea, he or she is willing to agree to the one the group discerns.

A Note About the Book

At Wellesley Meeting, Massachusetts, adults and children meet each Sunday before meeting in All Ages Religious Education (AARE). We hear a story or someone speaks about their faith journey. For about fifteen minutes, we discuss the story together. Then the children meet in their Sunday School classes, and adults continue the discussion downstairs. We have become a multigenerational community.

At one of these discussions, the children asked that they have a real junior meeting for business. They want to know what is going on at the meeting that might affect them and to have a say in those decisions. Nancy and David Haines serve as mentors, appointed by Ministry and Counsel. They are not their religious education teachers. This lets the children know that meeting for business is different and important to the life of the whole meeting.

The children range in age from seven to about thirteen. They are learning by doing. They appoint a clerk and a recording clerk, not necessarily the oldest children. We have had a twelve year old clerk and a ten year old clerk and both have done very well. We usually email the clerk in advance of the meeting and remind her or him to make an agenda. We meet with the clerk for a few minutes on the day of junior meeting for business. During the business meeting we may whisper to the clerks to remind them what to do.

For some topics, such as having a fundraising project or nominating a new clerk, the junior business meeting may appoint a working group or committee to do the work. This committee calls on the adults in the meeting as necessary for help.

The younger children, especially, get restless, so the meetings last about twenty to thirty minutes. We keep paper and crayons handy. Sometimes the meeting is a bit chaotic and sometimes a child can be disruptive. An older child has often stepped up to ask a younger child to be quiet or to suggest an activity. When we know there will be a particularly active child, we may request that another adult be present to help. It rarely goes as smoothly as the meeting in the story, but the children are proud that the meeting trusts them to make decisions for their community, and they try to follow good Quaker process.

The clerks of the junior business meeting occasionally report to the adult business meeting about their decisions and activities. We all are enriched by the work of our children.

Approved! was written with
the support of Wellesley Monthly Meeting
and published with a grant from the meeting.

For many years, New England Yearly Meeting has
included children's meeting for business as part of
the Annual Sessions program and elementary retreats
in the firm belief that children are quite capable of
participating in Quaker process.
We have all benefited from their experience.

Made in the USA
Columbia, SC
22 September 2021

45992770R00015